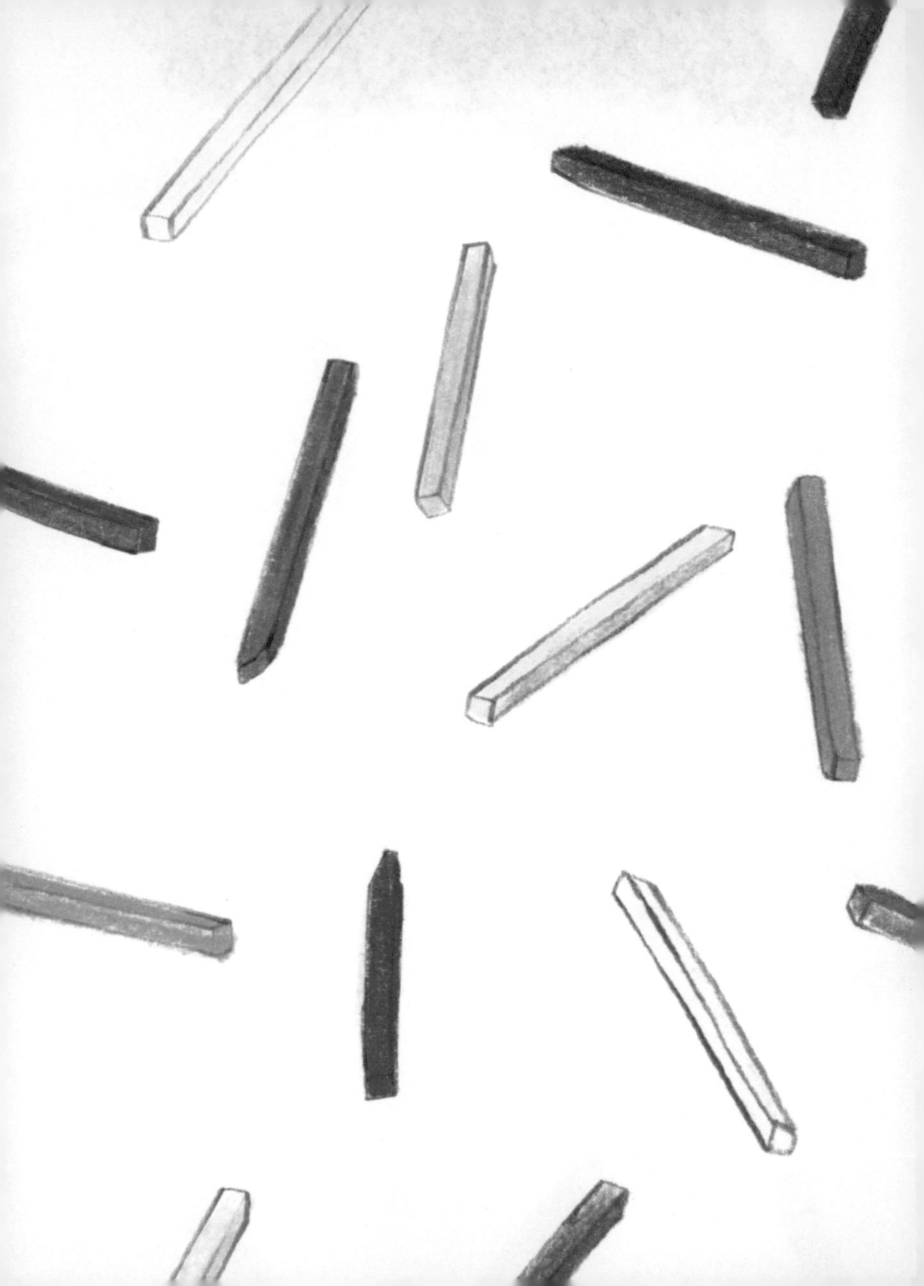

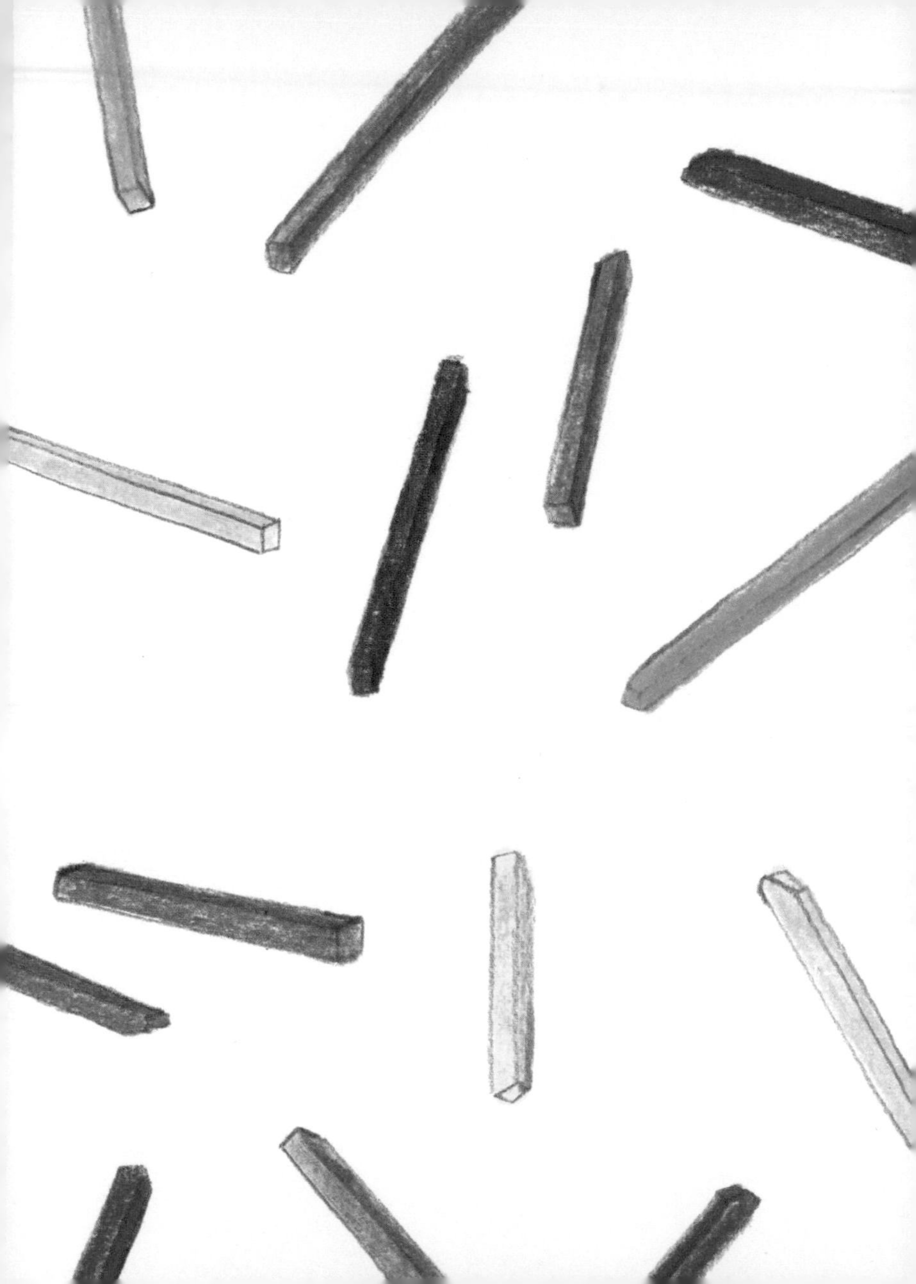

Elisabeth and the Box of COLOURS

Elisabeth and the Box of COLOURS

KATHERINE WOODFINE

With illustrations by
REBECCA COBB

Barrington Stoke

First published in 2022 in Great Britain by
Barrington Stoke Ltd
18 Walker Street, Edinburgh, EH3 7LP

www.barringtonstoke.co.uk

A CIP catalogue record for this book is available from the British Library upon request

ISBN: 978-1-80090-086-8

Printed by Hussar Books, Poland

This book is in a super-readable format for young readers beginning their independent reading journey.

For all the young artists and storytellers – K.W. & R.C.

Contents

Chapter 1

In a Tall House in Paris

Many years ago, in a tall house in Paris, there lived a girl called Elisabeth.

Elisabeth lived with her family – her papa, her mama and her baby brother, Etienne. Their house was always busy, full of cheerful noise and laughter.

Elisabeth's papa was an artist. He wore a blue coat that was covered in spots of paint. He spent every day working in his messy studio at the very top of the house.

Elisabeth loved nothing more than sitting in a corner, watching him work. He let her use his crayons, his paints and his brushes, and she spent hours making her own pictures of everything she saw.

Elisabeth drew their tall house with its green shutters and pots of red flowers. She drew the kitchen table with its blue and white cloth and the brown jug full of yellow roses. She drew the view she could see from the windows – the rooftops and spires.

But one day, everything changed. Elisabeth learned she would be going away to school.

Chapter 2

Off to School

Elisabeth was excited about going away to school. Mama said she would make new friends. Papa told her there would be lots to learn.

Soon, her bags were packed.

Mama put in Elisabeth's favourite blue dress and a new pink hair ribbon.

Papa tucked in a special parcel wrapped in brown paper. Inside was a drawing book and a box of Papa's very best coloured crayons. "So you can keep drawing," he whispered.

It was time to go. Elisabeth hugged Papa and Mama and Etienne goodbye, and then climbed into the carriage. She waved to them all from the window.

Her new school was only on the other side of Paris. But to Elisabeth it felt like she was setting out on a journey to the other side of the world.

Chapter 3

Elisabeth's New School

The first thing Elisabeth noticed about her new school was that everything was grey.

The school building was grey, and the yard outside it was grey too.

Inside, the classroom was grey, and the dormitory where she would sleep was grey. Even the dresses the schoolgirls wore were grey.

The girls sat in neat rows in front of their teacher, Sister Augustine. There was no talking or laughing. When one of them let out the smallest whisper or giggle, Sister Augustine frowned and said, "*Sshhh!*"

Sister Augustine unpacked Elisabeth's bags. She shook her head when she saw the blue dress and the pink hair ribbon. "You can't wear these here," Sister Augustine said, and took them away.

She shook her head again when she saw what was inside Papa's parcel. "Coloured crayons are against the rules," she said.

Elisabeth tried to explain. She wanted to say that Papa had told her to keep drawing. But Sister Augustine swept up Elisabeth's crayons. She locked them away in her big cupboard without another word.

Chapter 4

Splashes of Colour

Elisabeth sat alone in the classroom in her grey school dress. Soon, she began to feel grey herself.

She missed Papa and Mama and Etienne. She missed cheerful noise and laughter. She missed sitting in Papa's studio and the view she could see from the windows. She missed green shutters and red flowers, blue dresses and pink ribbons.

As the days passed, Elisabeth felt greyer than ever. She felt grey while she tried to work at her sums and her spellings. At playtime, she felt too grey to join in with the games of the other girls in the yard.

The greyness seemed to surround her like a cloud. But however grey she felt, there was one thing that always made Elisabeth feel better – a tiny splash of colour.

It might be a shiny red apple on her plate at suppertime. Or the green leaves of the tree she could see from the classroom window. A pink cloud

in the sky at sunset. A yellow butterfly. A stripy orange cat walking along the schoolyard wall.

Even the smallest flash of colour lifted her heart.

Sister Augustine had taken away Elisabeth's box of crayons, but she still had her drawing book. She also had the pen and ink she used in class.

Elisabeth began drawing what she saw. She drew clouds and leaves, cats and butterflies. And once she had started drawing, she found she could not stop.

It wasn't the same without her crayons. Elisabeth had no colours – only black ink. But even so, the pages of her drawing book became crowded with pictures. Soon, there wasn't even the tiniest blank space left.

Chapter 5

A Night-time Adventure

Now Elisabeth began to draw on the pages of her school books.

At first, Sister Augustine did not notice what she was doing. When the teacher looked over, she saw Elisabeth scribbling in her book. She thought that Elisabeth must be working very hard indeed.

But the other girls soon guessed that Elisabeth was up to something. They gave each other curious glances when Sister Augustine's back was turned.

Clara saw the teacher was busy helping Anna with her sums, so she leaned over to look at what Elisabeth was doing. Her eyes widened when she saw her book full of wonderful drawings. Soon, Clara had told all the other girls about what she had seen.

In the dormitory that night, Sylvie lit a candle. The girls crowded around Elisabeth's bed. "Can we see more of your pictures?" they asked. "Will you draw something for me?"

Elisabeth nodded. "But I don't have anything to draw with," she said.

Clara was the boldest of the schoolgirls – and she knew where Sister Augustine kept the key to her big cupboard. She crept out in the dark and tiptoed down the passage to the classroom. She opened the cupboard door, trying not to let it make even the smallest creak.

Inside, Clara found the box of crayons. She hurried back to the dormitory with them hidden inside her dressing gown.

Elisabeth was thrilled to have Papa's crayons back. Soon, she was busy drawing pictures for everyone.

She drew whatever the girls wanted. Animals for Clara, who missed her cat and dog. Flowers and trees for Anna, who was homesick for the countryside and the farm where she lived with her family. Wonderful hats and dresses for Sylvie, whose mama was a dressmaker. Magnificent cakes for Marie, whose papa was a baker.

The girls were delighted with their colourful pictures. They kept them hidden away inside the plain covers of their school books.

Little by little, school did not seem so grey after all.

Chapter 6

No More Drawing

It did not take Sister Augustine long to discover what Elisabeth had been doing. One day, she opened Elisabeth's book and found that the pages were covered with drawings, not sums. She looked inside Elisabeth's desk and found the box of crayons hidden there.

Sister Augustine was angry. “No more drawing!” she said, and took the crayons away again. “You must learn your lessons like everyone else!”

As a punishment, Elisabeth had only bread and water for supper. The other girls felt very sorry for her.

Now the pages of Elisabeth's school books were covered only in sums and spellings. Her fingers itched to draw on them, but she knew that Sister Augustine was watching her.

Instead, Elisabeth drew with her fingertip in the mist on a windowpane. And outside in the schoolyard, she found a stick and drew in the mud.

Chapter 7

Darkness Falls

One winter morning, Sister Augustine called Elisabeth into the classroom alone.

The teacher's face was serious and sad. Elisabeth wondered if she was in trouble again.

But then Sister Augustine said in a soft voice, “I am very sorry, Elisabeth. I have some bad news for you.”

Something terrible had happened in the tall house on the other side of Paris. Her papa had been taken ill – and then he had died.

Elisabeth’s world was plunged into darkness.

All the colour vanished. Now there was only grey, going on and on as far as she could see.

Chapter 8

Grey Days

Elisabeth went home for Papa's funeral. She travelled across the city in the carriage. From the window, she saw that the streets and rooftops of Paris were white with snow.

When she arrived home, she found that the green shutters were closed tightly. Inside, the door to Papa's studio was shut and locked. There were no cheerful voices and no laughter. Everything was silent and sad.

Elisabeth went back to school after the funeral. She sat at her desk, lost in a grey fog. The other girls tried to comfort her, and even Sister Augustine was kind. But Elisabeth did not notice.

The grey had crept right inside Elisabeth. It was there when she went to sleep at night, and there when she woke in the morning. Days passed, and still the whole world was grey.

In the dormitory, she lay awake. She tried to remember every detail of Papa's face. She wanted to remember everything about him – the way his eyes sparkled, the pattern of paint smears on his blue coat, the sound of his laugh. She was afraid she might forget.

Weeks passed. Spring was coming to Paris, and the birds were beginning to sing in the trees again.

But Elisabeth did not notice. She felt as grey as the clouds in the sky and the melting snow in the streets. Elisabeth felt so grey that it was as if she had turned invisible.

But she hadn't. The other girls were watching her. And Sister Augustine was watching too.

Chapter 9

An Unexpected Gift

In the dormitory that night, Sylvie lit a candle. Clara tiptoed over to Elisabeth's bed. "We've got a surprise for you!" she whispered.

In the orange light of the candle flame, Elisabeth saw something lying on the grey blanket. Surprised, she rubbed her eyes.

It was a handful of drawing supplies. But these were not like Papa's pastel crayons. There were a few broken chalks and a sticky old bottle of ink from the classroom. There were two pieces of charcoal rescued from the fire.

To draw on, there was an old school book, a few crumpled sheets of newspaper and a roll of brown paper.

Elisabeth stared – and the other girls watched her. "We collected them

for you," Anna said. "So you can start drawing your pictures again."

"We thought that perhaps drawing would help you feel better," said Marie.

"They aren't as good as *real* crayons," Clara said. "But they're better than nothing! And *this* time we'll hide them where Sister Augustine won't find them!"

Elisabeth looked at the heap of drawing things and then at the girls' faces, bright in the candlelight.

She smiled.

Chapter 10

Papa's Portrait

The next day, Elisabeth began to draw for the first time in many weeks. She used the ink and chalk and charcoal that the girls had given her.

She drew a portrait of Papa.

She tried to draw him as she remembered him best – cheerful and laughing in his messy studio.

It was very hard to draw with only a few broken chalks. The charcoal smudged and the sticky old ink blotted and smeared.

But little by little, Papa's face began to appear on the page.

Elisabeth worked on the portrait for a long time. When she had finished, she stared down at it, frowning. If only she had some colours to use – brown for Papa's hair, blue for his jacket, and red and green and yellow for the spots of paint!

Without colours, the picture wasn't right. But she set it away carefully in her desk anyway.

Chapter 11

The Box of Colours

It wasn't until the next morning that Elisabeth opened her desk again. When she lifted the lid, she saw something that made her gasp with amazement.

Lying beside her picture was a small parcel wrapped in brown paper. It was exactly like the one that Papa had given her when she'd first come to school.

Elisabeth's trembling fingers reached out for the parcel. Carefully, she unwrapped the paper. Inside, she found a new drawing book. Beside it were Papa's coloured crayons!

It was like magic. Elisabeth took out her picture again and went to work.

She used rich brown and yellow for Papa's hair. She used deep blue and purple for his coat, and covered it in colourful spots of paint. For his messy studio, she used a rainbow of bright colours.

Now the portrait seemed to glow with warmth and light. There was her papa, exactly as Elisabeth remembered him – cheerful, busy and laughing. Her heart felt full of happiness and sadness all at once.

She stared at the portrait for a long time. Then she put down her crayons and looked up at the classroom window.

Outside she could see the first new green leaves appearing on the tips of the trees' branches. A small yellow butterfly fluttered across a patch of pale blue sky.

Chapter 12

The Portrait Painter

Elisabeth showed the other girls her picture of Papa. They all crowded round to admire it.

Soon, the girls were telling her all about the people *they* loved best – their families and friends. They asked for portraits of their own. From then on,

Elisabeth drew portraits whenever a girl's family came to visit the school.

She drew Clara's brother with his dog at his side, and Anna's sister holding the flowers she had brought from the garden. She drew Sylvie's mama in a wonderful new dress and hat, and Marie's papa with the magnificent cake he had baked for them all.

That was how Elisabeth became a portrait artist. She was very clever at

drawing every detail of each person's face – but it was more than that. She had a gift for capturing what was special about the people she drew. Each of her pictures shone with warmth and light.

Soon, all the girls had colourful portraits of their family and friends hidden inside the plain covers of their school books. But that wasn't all.

Elisabeth made tiny drawings for the girls. They were so small they could keep them in their pockets or under their pillows.

She painted pictures on the walls of the dormitory, tucked away in secret corners where no one would notice them.

There were pictures in the girls' desks and hiding in cupboards behind their coats and hats.

Elisabeth used the big roll of brown paper the girls had given her to make an enormous picture. It was a portrait of all the schoolgirls together. At night in

the dormitory, they'd stick the picture up on the wall, transforming the grey room into a rainbow of colour. The girls worked on it together, talking and laughing as they drew.

The girls were always careful to be quiet so that Sister Augustine would not hear them. They kept their pictures tucked away, out of sight.

But Elisabeth was not sure they needed to be quite so careful any longer. She had an idea of where the brown paper parcel she'd found in her desk might have come from.

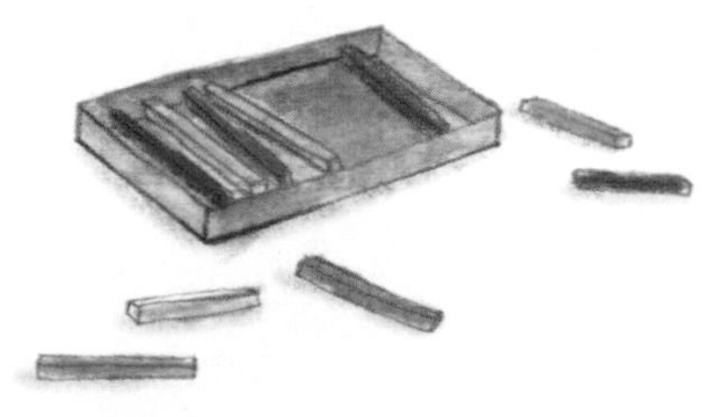

And once or twice, she thought she saw a twinkle in Sister Augustine's blue eyes that she'd never noticed before.

Elisabeth hung her drawings of her own family in the corner beside her bed in the dormitory. There was Mama and Etienne and her portrait of Papa. Every night before she went to sleep, she smiled at him and wished him goodnight.

She knew now that she would always miss Papa, but she would never forget him. The portrait helped her to remember him – cheerful and busy and laughing. She saw how her pictures helped the other girls to feel close to the people they missed too.

Elisabeth still felt sad. But she did not feel grey any longer.

The classroom was still quiet, and the schoolyard was still bare and cold, but school did not feel grey any more either.

It might *seem* grey. But Elisabeth knew that it was full of colour – if you only knew where to look.

Chapter 13

A World Full of Colour

The following years were not always easy for Elisabeth. There were things that happened that made her feel sad and grey and alone once more.

Even when she left school, there were still times when she felt like she had been swallowed up by a grey cloud.

Even when she became a famous painter just like her papa – with a studio of her own that was just as messy and wonderful as his had been.

But Elisabeth knew now that her work could help to comfort her – and other people too. She had her crayons and paintbrushes at hand, and the help of people she cared about. The clouds would pass eventually. No matter how grey things might seem, the world would shine brightly with colour once again.

About the Real Élisabeth Vigée Le Brun

This story is inspired by Élisabeth Louise Vigée Le Brun. She was born in 1755 and grew up to become a world-famous artist.

Élisabeth loved drawing from a very young age. She went away to school at six years old and often got in trouble for drawing on her school books and even on the walls of her dormitory. But her father, Louis Vigée, was an artist and saw that she was very talented. He knew that she would become a painter one day.

In this story, Elisabeth's father dies while she is away at school. In real life, Louis Vigée died when Élisabeth was twelve, shortly after she had left school.

Élisabeth felt unable to paint and draw for a time. But she soon returned to making art as a way to help her cope with her "sad thoughts".

Élisabeth kept on drawing and painting. By the age of fifteen, she had set up her own studio and was painting portraits professionally. She was young and had no formal art training, but she quickly became very successful. She painted many of the most important people in Paris. She even became one of very few female members of the French Royal Academy.

In 1778, Élisabeth was invited to the Palace of Versailles to paint Queen Marie Antoinette. She soon became the queen's favourite painter, as well as her close friend. Élisabeth went on to paint over thirty portraits of the queen.

When the French Revolution began, Élisabeth and her daughter, Julie, escaped from Paris. They travelled across Europe, living in Italy, Russia and Germany, and Élisabeth continued her career as a portrait artist.

Today her work can be found in art galleries and museums all over the world. She is remembered as one of France's most important painters.

Our books are tested
for children and young people by
children and young people.

Thanks to everyone who consulted on
a manuscript for their time and effort in
helping us to make our books better
for our readers.

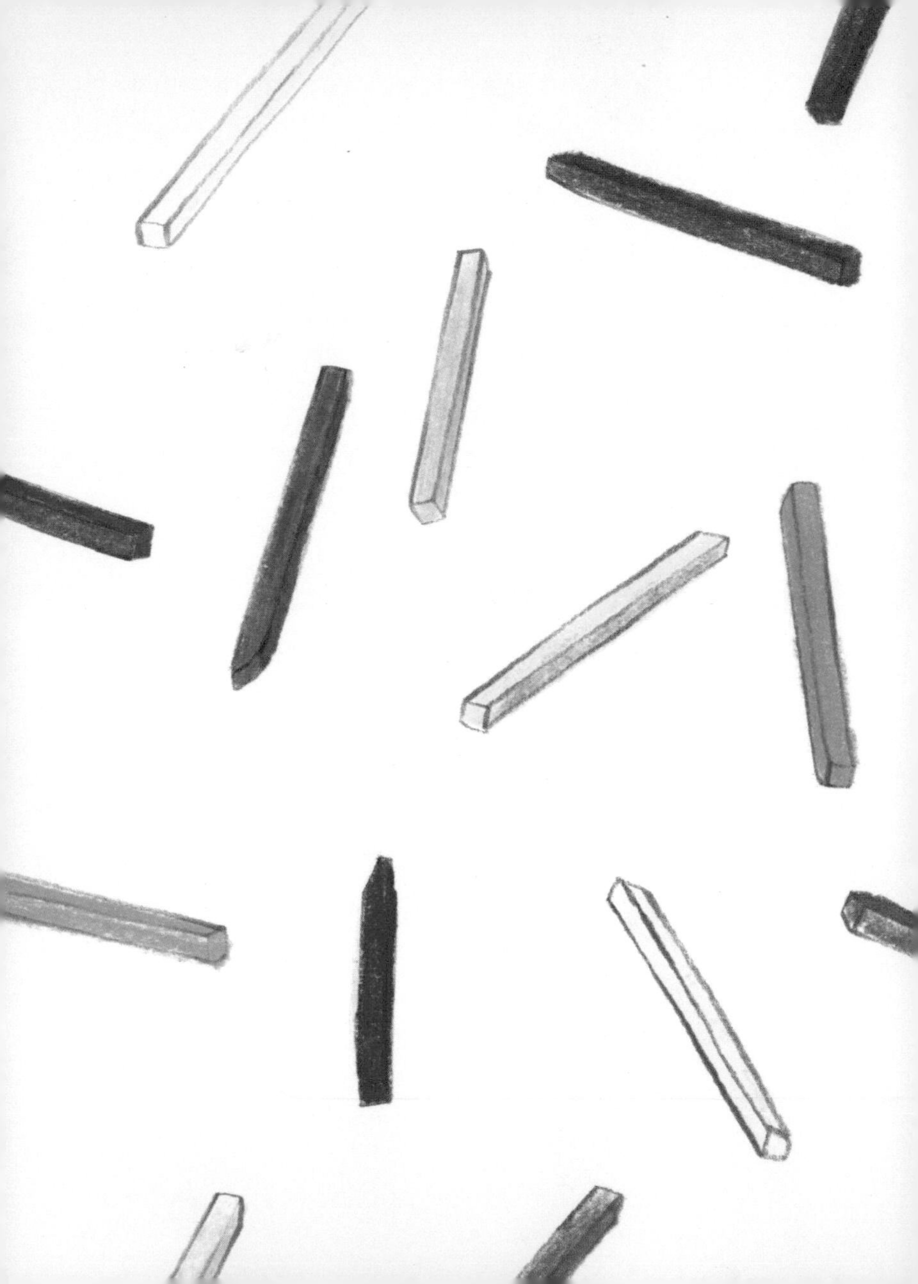